My Child...

All scriptures are taken from the New Living Translation

Life Application Study Bible, Second Edition.

PALMETTO
PUBLISHING
Charleston, SC
www.PalmettoPublishing.com

Paperback ISBN: 9798822960091

My Child...

WRITTEN BY
Annairis Perkins

ILLUSTRATED BY
Mason Perkins & Makayla Perkins

My Child...

A book that shares words of the heart and the prayers of a

mother to and for her child through the eyes of God.

Words of affirmation and Bible verses included.

Acknowledgments

To God:

You said: "'For I know the plans I have for you, says the Lord. They are plans for good and not for disaster, to give you a future and a hope.'"(Jeremiah 29:11). Thank you. Lord, I thank you for every tear, every lesson, every roadblock, every struggle, and every trial. Thank you for allowing me to prosper, thank you for your healing touch, and thank you for giving me hope and a future. God, I thank you.

Dear Raymond,

I wanted to take a moment to express my deepest gratitude to you. Your unwavering support and encouragement have meant the world to me as I've pursued my dreams. Thank you for always standing right by my side. I'm so thankful to have you as my husband.

With all my love,

Your Dear

To my father:

Thank you for always believing in me and instilling in me that I could do anything I wanted to in this life and to not let anyone tell me any different. Your optimism, strength, and resilience have always been encouraging and exemplary.

Love you always, Daddy.

To my mother:

Thank you for introducing me to God by taking and forcing me to go to church even when I didn't want to. It was your actions that have created the pathway for me to come to know God for myself today!

The Bible says in Proverbs 22:6, "Direct your children onto the right path, and when they are older, they will not leave it." Mom, I have not departed, and when the storms of life are raging over me, in the rock I know to hide!

Love you always, Mommy.

To Ms. Abraham:

You cared, you listened, you nurtured, you mentored, you prayed, you believed, you loved, you taught, and you stayed. You've taught me that everything in life is driven by perspective, and if I can change my perspective on any situation, I can always make it work for me.

Thus the outcomes in my life are built on the foundation of my perspective.

Ben Franklin said, "Well done is better than well said."

You have done well; well done, Ms. A., well done!

May your life be filled with joy, may you experience an abundance of love, and may the recognition of God's presence fill you with peace.

May everything that you so desire come to pass; may you never lack for any good thing. May your heart never ache from the worries of this world; may your faith never grow weary in his ability to carry you. May every angel of glory show up above, below, around, and on every side of your life, because you have done well.

Amen and Amen.

My Child,

You are the child I have always longed for, the mini-me I've always imagined; you are the apple of my eye; you are the fruit of my womb. May you always know that you were wanted and that you matter. May you always know that you are beautiful. May you always know that you are enough. May you always know that you are who God says that you are. May you always know that you were created by God in his image and likeness. May you always know whose and who you are. May you always know that I love you! May you always know that God loves you!

God says in Job 33:4: "For the Spirit of God has made me, and the breath of the Almighty gives me life."

My Child,

You are my bright and morning star. You are my light bright. My bright light: in the midst of darkness, you shine in every room. May you always know that you are the head and not the tail. A leader and not a follower, above and not beneath. A lender and not a borrower. May you always know that God created you with a purpose. May you always know that you are capable of doing any and all things. May you never allow others or the world to dim your dreams and imaginations. May you always seek and trust God in all you do so that he may give you guidance. May you always soar high and accomplish excellence in all you do.

God says you can do all things in Philippians 4:13: "For I can do everything through Christ, who gives me strength."

God says: Trust him, and he will guide your steps.

Proverbs 3:5–6: "Trust in the Lord with all your heart; do not depend on your own understanding. Seek his will in all you do, and he will show you which path to take."

My Child,

May you live life with confidence and freedom. May you live life with fearlessness. May you live life with faith, may you live life with resilience, and may you live life without regrets. May you always know that no matter what you do, no matter how far you go, or no matter how old you grow, I will always love you. May you live life with only learned lessons. May you live life with gratitude and appreciation. May you live life with wisdom, kindness, love, forgiveness, understanding, and a heart of peace.

May God continually make the devil a liar in your life. May you never want for anything. May the favor of the Lord be upon you. May you always find refuge in the name of Jesus.

God says: I will give you rest. Matthew 11:28: "'Then Jesus said, 'Come to me, all of you who are weary and carry heavy burdens, and I will give you rest.'"

My Child,

May you always know that no matter what happens in your life, you have the power to decide how you respond to each situation. Your thoughts determine your perspective, and your perspective will determine your outcome. So may you always think and speak positivity into yourself. May you always surround yourself with positivity. When tough moments happen in your life, may you always know that with God all things are possible. May you always know that God is able. May you always remember that God will take care of all your needs. May you always remember that God will give you peace. May you always know that God will never leave you. May you always remember to call on him, pray to him, seek him, and he will guide you and bring you rest.

God says: I will supply your needs. Philippians 4:19: "And this same God who takes care of me will supply all your needs from his glorious riches, which have been given to us in Christ Jesus."

God says: I will never leave you or forsake you. Hebrews 13:5: "Don't love money; be satisfied with what you have. For God has said, 'I will never fail you. I will never abandon you.'

Be Still And Know
That I Am
God

My Child,

May you know, may you see, may you experience, and may you feel that life is filled with joy, happiness, pleasure, blessings, and the favor of the Lord. When the struggles of life challenge you—and they will—may the wisdom of God remind you that "The righteous person faces many troubles, but the Lord comes to the rescue each time." (Psalm 34:19). Remember that afflictions are the issues of life, and problems will arise, but when they do, please know that the peace and grace of God is enough to keep you through any situation. May you embrace a solution-focused mindset that will allow you to think clearly and tackle any problem that arises along with the guidance of God. May you be still and know that he is God. May the word of God remind you in 2 Timothy 1:7: "For God has not given us a spirit of fear and timidity, but of power, love, and self discipline."

My Child,

May you know that your life is a journey and that it is meant for you to live, learn, and experience the blessings and power of God. May you know that the path through your journey may not always be straight; it may not always be clear; in fact, it may sometimes be confusing and frustrating. You will sometimes make mistakes, and that is okay. What's most important as you figure life out is that you seek and put God before anything you do in prayer and that you learn and grow from your errors. May you always know that there isn't anything you can do that will cause God's love for you to change. God is love, and he loves you! God's love is unconditional, his love is gentle, his love is pure, his love is healing, and his love is forever. May you know that no matter what it looks, feels, or seems like, God will always work each and every situation out in your life for your good.

God says in Romans 8:28, "And we know that God causes everything to work together for the good of those who love God and are called according to his purpose for them."

My Child,

May you know that when God moves on your behalf, he will do it to perfection. It will be all your heart has desired and more. May you not force or rush things in your life but rather be patient and trust God's timing and ability to act on your behalf. May you understand and know that everything happens when it's supposed to happen and how it's supposed to happen. So, my child, don't worry and trust God, as he is omnipresent, everlasting, and all-powerful. He moves mountains, and he can move each and every mountain that you encounter. May you know that God is always a prayer and a conversation away. May you know that your constant and unwavering relationship, faith, and obedience with and to God is your road map to living a life that's pleasing unto the sight of God.

Jeremiah 29:11: "'For I know the plans I have for you, says the Lord. 'They are plans for good and not for disaster, to give you a future and a hope.'"

My Child,

May you be in the world but not of it. May you be stable in your thoughts and in all your ways.

May you know and go the way of the Lord. May you not be confused by the calamity of the world.

May you walk like a child of God, may you speak like a child of God, may you love like a child of God, and may you forgive like a child of God. May you fear the Lord, may you trust him, and may you live a life that is pleasing to God. May you know and understand that it is impossible to please man, but you can please God through faith, reverence, and obedience to him.

May the word of God remind you in Hebrews 11:6: "And it is impossible to please God without faith. Anyone who wants to come to him must believe that God exists and that he rewards those who sincerely seek him."

May the word of God remind you in Romans 8:8: "That's why those who are still under the control of their sinful nature can never please God."

My Child,

May you know that God will supply your every need. No matter what it looks like, feels like, or sounds like, the Bible says in Philippians 4:19, "And this same God who takes care of me will supply all your needs from his glorious riches, which have been given to us in Christ Jesus." When the storms of life come raging over you, know that you have to lean on God. Align yourself with God—all you have to do is talk to him. Your prayers are just talks with God. He hears you, and he's listening to you. God answers prayers, but you have to believe in him. Please do not worry, please do not stress, please do not take matters into your own hands, and please do not force things in your life. The word of God also tells us in Philippians 4:6-7: "Don't worry about anything; instead, pray about everything. Tell God what you need, and thank him for all he has done. Then you will experience God's peace, which exceeds anything we can understand. His peace will guard your hearts and minds as you live in Christ Jesus."

Psalm 30:5: "For his anger lasts only a moment, but his favor lasts a lifetime! Weeping may last through the night, but joy comes with the morning."

My Child,

I pray that the angels of the Lord surround you on every side. I pray that you experience the joys that come from knowing and following God. May your ears only hear the victories of God, may your eyes only see the goodness of God, and may you receive an abundance of love. May you only experience the beauty of God's love. May the calling on your life cause you to be the light in the midst of darkness. As I bind the spirit of fear, doubt, and evil against your life, I pray that God grants you a spirit of peace, love, and a sound mind. I pray against every plan of the enemy over your mind, your body, and your spirit.

I declare that your mind will be sober, aligned, and hungry for the things and the word of God. I declare that your body will be healthy and whole. I pray that you will always feel the presence of God in your life. I pray that his presence encamps around you like a shield, guarding you from the hand of the enemy. May your faith in God cause you to live in confidence and be an inspiration to those around you. May you walk in the light of love, may you be the owner and not the employee, may you be the chosen one and not the picked, may you be a good friend, may you be a good person, and may you be respectful, kind, and loving to others. May your mouth speak good and truth. May you help and not hurt, may you love and not hate, may you bless and not curse, and may the power of God carry, keep, protect, and guide you both now and forevermore.

In Jesus's name, let us declare a loud: Amen.

A message from the Illustrators:

We want you to remember that no matter how old you are, or what challenges you may face in life, with God you can do all things. Thank you for reading our family book and we hope your heart was blessed and encouraged.

- Mason and Makayla

Milton Keynes UK
Ingram Content Group UK Ltd.
UKRC031101021174
4503681UK00001B/4

* 9 7 9 8 8 2 2 9 6 0 0 9 1 *